Clay's
Battle Between
True Love and Lust

Clay's Battle Between True Love and Lust

GEORGE MILLS

ISBN: 978-1-965679-70-8 (sc)
ISBN: 978-1-965679-71-5 (e)

Rev. date: 01/07/2025

"Clay, are you going with us to John's son Mork's for supper tonight?"

"No, Mrs. Mary, I'm feeling the need to have a talk with Lana...that if she doesn't mind talking with me."

"No, Clay, I don't mind at all having a talk with you."

"Wait now, Lana, I was hoping that you and Lawrence were going with us, for there's something that John and I need to talk with you all about tonight."

"Mother, can't you and John just tell us here?"

"Well, John, should we just tell them here?"

"Yes, Mary, we might as well tell them now."

"Okay then. John, would you prefer me to tell them, or would you like to be the one?"

"Mary, I'll tell them. Lana, Lawrence, we've decided to sell everything and do some traveling."

Lawrence looked at his mother and said, "Wow, Mom, when did you both decide on doing that?"

"Lawrence, we decided this about two weeks ago, and John is going to let Clay rent the shop so he'll have a place to live...that's if John's two sons are okay with him doing that."

"Mom."

"Yes, Lana."

"If you're needing a place to storage your personal stuff, you can use my storage shed."

"Yes, Mom, you and John are welcome to use mine as well."

"Thank you both for your kind offer. I have some of your father's things that I would love for you both to keep for me while we're away. Now look, don't everyone go get all emotional. They're not going to stay gone forever."

"Hmm, that's what you think, Clay. Wait, you may be right. If you don't send me the rent payment on my shop, I'll be back."

"John, if we're going to Mork's, we need to be on our way."

"Yes, my dear, you're right. We will see you all sometime tomorrow afternoon."

"Okay, John, Mom. We love you both."

"We love you both as well. Good night."

"Lana, we need to be going as well."

"Okay, Lawrence. Be careful going home."

*****

"Man, I was beginning to think they would never leave."

"Clay, did you just say something?"

"No, ma'am, I was only thinking out loud."

"Oh, okay, then what do you need to talk with me about?"

"Lana, would you mind taking a walk with me down to the beach? There's where I do my best thinking?"

"What about your ankle? Are you sure you're up to taking that long walk?"

"I'll put on the boot that the doctor gave me, and it should be fine."

"Okay, hardhead, it's your choice, but I believe we can talk here just as well as we could down at the beach."

"Well, how about you let me try walking around with the boot on first before you go calling me hardheaded?"

"Well, how does it feel walking with the boot?"

"I must say it doesn't feel that great at all. It's like walking on the side of a hill."

"You got to use the crutches that he gave you. I now understand why John calls you a big dummy."

"Oh, okay. Not only am I hardheaded, but I'm also dumb."

"No, don't take what I said the wrong way, for that's not what I mean."

"Well then, how am I to take what you said?"

"Just not in the way it sounded. I spoke without thinking. Will you please forgive me?"

"Lana, there's no way that I can hold anything against you...especially that anyways...and you're right, we can talk here as good as at the beach."

"Thank you. Now what would you like to talk with me about, Clay?"

"Well now, Lana, it's about love and lust. Are you okay talking about the two?"

"Well, it depends on just how deep you're wanting to get with the subject."

Hmm, I wonder why she thinks there's nothing deep about the subject.

 "Clay, why do you have that puzzled look on your face? Did I say something wrong?"

"No, you didn't. I was only thinking as to where I wanted to start the conversation. I guess I'll start by asking this question—no, wait, before I go asking any questions, I need to bring you up-to-date as to what had been going on in my life."

"Well, Clay, that would be a good place to start."

"I'll start by saying Mary Ann has confessed her love for me, and I myself, in return, told her that I felt the same way toward her. But now that some time has passed between us telling each other how we feel, I'm left only to wonder if it's true love or only lust that we're feeling for each other. As you may or may not know, it has been a very long time since each of us had been in a real relationship. Just last night, she had me over for dinner, and she was wearing this tight blue sleeping shirt that only came halfway down her beautiful sexy thighs, which left me in disbelief. When I got ready to leave, she asked if I thought she was evil."

"Now, Clay, what is wrong with her wearing that? You both are grown adults, are you not?"

"Yes, we both are grown adults."

"Okay then, tell me where the problem is in her wearing the sleeping shirt."

"Lana, the problem lies within the temptation that came from her showing off more than what I needed to see."

"So, am I to believe that you, Clay, of all people, can't handle seeing a beautiful woman wearing nothing but her sleeping shirt? My oh my, now what is this world coming to?"

I'm starting to believe that she's not everything that Mrs. Mary says she is because if she was, I don't believe she would be talking the way she is right now.

"Well, Lana, I'm not sure as to how to answer that question. So let's be moving right along with this conversation on understanding what the difference is between love and lust."

"Hey, is this conversation going to be about you learning what the difference is between true love and lust?"

"Yes, Lana...well, maybe not the entire conversation. I'm kinda hoping by us having this discussion, I could get to know more about you. That's why I'm asking you for your help."

"Hmm, are you saying that you're interested in getting to know more about me?"

"Yes, ma'am, I'm guessing in a roundabout way, I am. Now is there a problem?"

"No, Clay, there's no problem. You just caught me off guard. Now what's your question?"

"Lana, what do you believe or feel is the difference between true love and lust?"

"Clay, I can't say I've ever given any thought to that subject. Now that you have asked, I would like to see just what Google has to say. Now it looks like there is a great deal of difference between the two of them."

"Oh, yes, it most definitely does, but it doesn't give me a definitive answer as to what I'm looking for."

"Well, Clay, if any of these doesn't answer your question, then I'm not sure how to help you."

"Hmm, let me ask the question in a different way and see what answer will come up. When a man sees a woman or a woman sees a man, what is the reason behind their attraction for one another?"

"Hmm, Clay, it's looking like we're getting the same answers as before."

"You're right, Lana, but I'm not going to stop searching for the best possible answer. What do you think about searching one or two of the answers?"

That find Lana. "Okay."

BATTLE BETWEEN TRUE LOVE AND LUST

"These are only two of the answers that was found on Google: (1) Findings suggest physical attraction is often the spark that inspires a connection between people. (2) The biological 'drive' of attraction is inherent to living and evolving systems and is the results of their inherent biological activities."I may or may not agree with biological 'drive' of attraction being the one I'm looking for, so before I agree, let's see what the definition is: 'The basic processes of life include organization, metabolism, responsiveness, movements, and reproduction. In humans, who represent the mast complex form of life, there are additional requirements such as growth, differentiation, respiration, digestion, and excretion. All of these processes are interrelated.'"Hmm, Lana, what's your thoughts on this being the right answer?"

"Well, to be completely honest, I would say it could go either way."

"Now, Lana, why do you say that?"

"Well, Clay it's like this. Let's say, for instance, that I find you to be very physically attractive and would love to get to know more about you and maybe one day I would say to you that I'd love to lay with you. Now, Clay, let me ask you this question. Now how would you describe that? Would it be love or lust?"

"Lana, I'd more likely say that if it's only a physical attraction you're feeling. Wait, before I answer you, keep this in mind."

"Keep what in mind, Clay?"

"Well, first, I must also find you physically attractive, Lana, and if I do, then I would say it's love."

"Yes, I agree with your answer, but what if you don't find me physically attractive? Then would it be lust or love on my part, Clay?"

"Look, now! Lana, that's the very question in which I'm trying to find the right answer to. Now why are you laughing?"

"I'm just laughing at the way you responded to my question."

"I'm thinking we need to turn to the Bible to look for some answers."

"Wait, Clay, before we go looking for more answers in the Bible, there's something you said earlier that has got me curious, and I'd like to know why you brought the subject up?"

"Yes, Lana, what would that have been?"

"Clay, you said that you would like to get to know more about me. Why is that?"

"Hmm, did I say that, Lana?"

"Yes, you did. Now don't go trying to deny saying it."

"Well, Lana, your mom has made mention to me time after time that when you call her, you're always asking how I'm doing, so I just thought maybe I should get to know more about you, that's all."

"Well, okay then, Clay, what would you like to know?"

Hmm, I'm thinking just how I start this conversation off. "Well, Lana, what about you start by telling me something that you really enjoy doing when you're not at work?"

"Okay, Clay. I love going fishing on a nice summer day... that's if the wind isn't blowing and I'm not having work in my flower garden. As you can see, I've one of the most beautiful flower gardens in the neighborhood."

"Yes, you do at that, and I can tell that the honeybees are loving it as well."

"Oh yes, I also have a bee farm that I keep up. Also, do you like honey?"

"Yes, Lana, I like honey a lot. Now what about you telling me something that's not all that obvious for someone like myself to pick up on when they meet you for the first time?"

"Wait, hold on, Clay, I'm not going to share that kind of information with you right now."

"What, Lana, did I ask the wrong question? If so, I'm sorry?"

"Clay, there are things that has happened in my life since my dad passed away that not even my mom or brothers even knows about. Now that's because I don't like to talk about my personal life to anyone."

"Lana, I wasn't trying to pry into your dear persons' private affairs at all. I only wanted to know if you ever had a boyfriend or not...that's all."

"Then, Clay, you should have just asked that. Yes, I had my share of boyfriends...more than I care to recall. It seems like every one of them, except one, were dirtbags, for they only wanted one thing from me. Clay, I'm telling you here and now, for I'm not that kind of woman who would sleep with just anyone just for the pleasure of doing so. Now would you like a cup of tea or coffee?"

"Yes, Lana, I would love a cup of coffee, thank you."

"Clay, here's your coffee."

"Lana, you did say all but one of your boyfriends were dirtbags. May I ask about that one?"

"Clay, he was the only one that ever treated me with any respect. He didn't try to get me into his bed. He and I had made plans to get married, but before we could get everything set in place to do so the company he was working for at the time offered him another position as a fulltime supervisor over in a different country. You know the saddest part of their offer was that they didn't even give him any other options—either he took it or he wouldn't have a job."

"Lana, I know how he must have felt, having to leave the woman he loves behind. Every time I had to leave my lovely wife and family behind to go off to war, it felt like my life had been torn in half."

"Well, Clay, you had a choice to join the military or not whereas he had no choice with the company he was working for."

"Oh, wait just a minute, Lana, am I understanding that you are comparing his job to me choosing to serve and protect the people which I love?"

"Well, no, Clay, that's not the way I meant to say what I was wanting to say."

"Well then, Lana, just what were you going to say?"

"Clay, right now I don't even remember as to what I was thinking. Can we please just change the subject...okay?"

"Lana, it has gotten late. Would you mind taking me back to Mr. John's."

"Yes, Clay, I will take you back. Just give me a few minutes to pack some clothes for the night."

I'm thinking as to why is she needing to pack her clothes. Surely she not going to stay the night at Mr. John's? "Okay, Clay, I'm ready. Do you need my help getting in the car again?"

"No, thanks, I got this. Wait, Lana, let me get my legs in before you go pulling off."

"Sorry! Clay, I thought you were all ready."

"No. Can't you see I'm not in the car yet?"

A RIDE WITH LANA

"Lana, why are you driving like you're on your way to fight a house fire?"

"Clay, if you don't like my driving, I'll be more than happy to let you walk."

Hmm, that might not be a bad idea. "No, I don't think I'd like walking that far, Lana, but will you please slow down? I'd love to live for another day."

"Oh, okay, crybaby, I'll slow down, but you're getting out."

"Look now, Lana, if there's anything I've said to make you this angry at me, I'm truly sorry. Please don't ask me to get out."

"Well then, you need to keep your watering hole shut until we get to Mr. John's."

Hmm, I know where she gets her attitude from—her mother.

*****

"Good evening, Mrs. Mary, Mr. John."

"Well, Clay, how did your talk with Lana go?"

"Mrs. Mary, I'm going to let her tell you I'm needing to speak with Mr. John."

"Lana, what was that all about?"

"Mom, can we talk about this later? I need to unpack my clothes."

"Well, Lana, I'm guessing it didn't go that great."

"Mom, I said we'll talk about this last, okay."

*****

"Clay, you said you had something you're wanting to talk with me about."

"Yes, sir, I do...that's if you and Mrs. Mary don't mind talking with me."

"Clay, you know that Mary and I don't mind talking with you. Now what's on your mind?"

"Mr. John, there's been, once again, this great question come before me, and I believe you and Mrs. Mary can help me find the answer to it."

"Hmm, Clay, in the way you just put it, that has gotten me wondering."

"Oh, Mr. John, there's no need for you to worry about this question. I've learned a lot from you and Mrs. Mary—great wisdom—since I've been staying here."

"Clay, we both have enjoying having you here, but don't you think you're putting way too much icing on our cake?"

"No, sir, I don't believe that I have. You and Mrs. Mary have been very charitable in helping me."

"Well now, does that mean we get to add you on our income taxes for the year?"

"Mr. John, that would be a *big no.*"

"Well then, what is this great question of yours?"

"Sir, the question is how can someone tell the difference between true love and lust?"

"Hmm, Clay, before I give you any advice, let me ask you this—just how are you planning on using the answer I give you?"

"I'm sorry, Mr. John, I'm not sure I fully understand your question."

"Let me ask it in a different way then and hope you'll understand. Are you going to use our answer as being a witness to someone or just for common knowledge for yourself?"

"Hmm, that's a good question that I've not thought of. I'm guessing, Mr. John, I could use it both ways if I find there's a need...unless you don't want me to."

"Okay then, I believe that's good enough, don't you, Mary?"

"Yes, John, that's good enough for me.""Okay now, let's stop talking and let me think about this for a minute or two. Clay, after doing some deep thinking in these two minutes, I believe if you're going to use this as a tool for witnessing to someone, you'll be getting very deep into a very, very important point in the process."

"Well, Mr. John, if that's all you could come up with in those two minutes, I believe I could have come up with that on my own."

"Clay, you know how you feel when someone interrupts you when you're talking?"

"Yes, sir, I do because you do it to me all the time."

"Good. Then stop interrupting me, and let me finish my conversation. As I was going to say, for someone like yourself, trying to offer guidance on these two words is going to be a great challenge for you. Now as to why I'm saying this, first, Clay, is because you know your own ability of using the correct grammar and pronunciation of words. That within itself will become your greatest downfall in any conversation you may have with someone. Wait before either of you say anything. I have more to say. Lust is a worldly gesture/feeling/act, and I'm sure there's other words I can't even think of right now because of Clay's interruption. I believe these all falls under 'biological drive.'

"For we know God gave us the world and heavenly feeling and desires to repopulate. I'm going to suggest when you get time, look in Genesis 1:28 and read what God had said. Now, Clay, as you well know, God also gave us rules and regulations to live by. When God 'made man in His own image,' this included choice, Clay. Are you understanding what I'm saying?"

"Yes, sir, I'm understanding you very well. Just because of my own inability to use those fancy words like you doesn't mean I don't understand them."

"Good, then I'll continue. Now I'll explain to you the ultimate goal is to understand God gave mankind the ability to reason, think, learn higher thinking levels. Now these are what makes the difference between the animal kingdom and human, which causes us to have to make choices."

"Wait, Mr. John, please don't misunderstand me, but I don't feel that you fully understood the question that I'd asked."

"Yes, John, I believe Clay is right...you didn't fully understand the question he asked."

"Mary, why are you agreeing with him? Have I not told you he's not all there mentally?"

"John, you ain't right for saying that about him. I've understood every word you've said, and even I haven't heard one word where you even came close to an answer to his question."

"If you both would stop interrupting me, you would get an answer."

"Okay, continue on, John."

"Thank you. Now this ability to make choices is the separation and definition of 'being created in God's image. This brings me back to love versus lust. Lust is worldly, is biologically driven, driven by Satan, and is plain wrong as I understand it. Love is used/abused by the world and by religion. We, as mankind, *hide* behind love while we're lusting like wild animals."

"Now, Mr. John, are you saying we're to base the difference between true love and lust only on the choices that we make in our everyday life?"

"Clay, I'm going to end by just saying this here. You could try writing a thousand-page book on this very subject, and you would never completely find/define/ explain the difference between love and lust. Just by the conclusion of the book would leave the reader having to search their own heart to make a choice. I believe

God made mankind to make these 'choices' rather than writing a hard definition as though some hotshot lawyer was arguing the case of 'love versus lust' in a courtroom. Now, Clay, Lana, you both are more than welcome to stay up as long as you like, but Mary and I are going to bed. Good night."

"Good night, Mom. Love you."

"I love you too, Lana."

"Lana, I'm so sorry for making you mad earlier."

"Clay, will you forget about it? I have now. Good night."

"Okay. Thank you and good night to you as well. As I'm getting ready for bed, everything that Mr. John had said about it being within the choices that we make starts to weigh heavy on my mind. Now as to what does come to my mind is the book of Job, for we know the story of what happened in Job's life, right? Okay, maybe you remember or maybe you don't...that's beside the point. Now you might also be asking yourself why the book of Job. Well, I'm fixing to tell you if you'll give me a minute to get to the right page in my KJV Bible. What I'm taking notice of in Job chapter 2:9–10 reads as follows: 'Then said his wife unto him, "Dost thou still retain thine integrity? Curse God and die." But he said unto her, "Thou speakest as one of the foolish women speaketh. What? Shall we receive good at the hand of God, and shall we not receive evil?" In all this did not Job sin with his lips.'

"Here's where I find that Mr. John is making his case about having a choice between true love and lust. Let's say I had to base my decision just from Job having a choice between true love and lust. I would say he chose true love over lust. Here's why I believe he loved God more than he loved his own life. Yes, one could say that's not so by saying he chose lust instead. Then ask this question—how could someone understand the thought process or consider something as serious as 'do I live, or do I curse God and die?' Let's me find where it says that God has no glory in the dead. Looking in the KJV, in the book of Psalm 115:15–18, it reads as follows: 'Ye are blessed of the Lord which made heaven and earth. The heaven, even the heavens, are the Lord's: but the earth hath he given to the children of men. The dead praise not the Lord, neither any that go down into silence. But we will bless the Lord from this time forth and for ever-more. Praise the Lord.'"Hmm, I now understand what Mr. John meant when he said God hath given the earth to the children of men. He said read Genesis chapter 1:28. I'm going to read that chapter and see just why he had referred it to me, and maybe there I'll find my answer. It reads as follows: KJV Genesis chapter 1:27: 'So God created man in his own image, in the image of God created he him; male and female created he them. And God blessed them, and God said unto them, "Be fruitful, and multiply, and replenish the earth, and subdue it: and have dominion over the fish of the sea, and over the fowl of the air, and over every living thing that moveth upon the earth."""

ONE'S UNDERSTANDING

"After reading this chapter in Genesis, I must say I understand every single part about God creating male and female in His own image and giving unto them the blessing of being fruitful and the ability to multiply and replenish the earth. But still yet, I feel as if I'm missing the very mark as to understanding the difference between true love and lust. Maybe if I give myself a little rest from searching for this answer that I so greatly desire to know and get a good night's sleep, perhaps tomorrow I'll able to see things a little different."

"Oh, Clay, it's time to get up. I got breakfast ready."

"Oh, please, Mrs. Mary, don't tell me it's that time already, for it feels as if I just closed my eyes for the first time tonight. I'm guessing this day is going to be no different than any other day around here. Oh, wait, there is one thing different. Miss Lana's here. Mrs.

Mary, I'm going to get a quick shower before I join y'all for breakfast."

"Clay, you're going to have to wait. Lana is already in the shower."

"Well, then, I hope she doesn't use up all the hot water like Mr. John does. Good morning to you both. Mr. John, I took your advice last night and read Genesis's chapter 1:27 and 28, but I still was unable to distinguish the difference between true love and lust."

"Clay, are you still searching for that answer?"

Yes, Mrs. Mary, I'm still searching for an answer. I'm hoping by the end of today I've one. Good morning, Miss Lana, how are you? Did you get a good night's sleep?"

"Yes, Clay, I got a good night's sleep."

"I must say you're looking very lovely this morning."

"Thank you, Clay."

"Oh, Lana, it's a pleasure to give such a beautiful woman as yourself a compliment."

"Clay, I thought you were going to take a shower."

"Yes, you're right, I am, Mr. John...right after I've finished my breakfast."

In that very moment, I could tell that something was wrong just by the way Mr. John turned and looked at Mrs. Mary after I'd said what I did, but I was unable to fully grasp the concept as to what was wrong. I know it could not have been what I'd said to Lana because from the first time I'd met Mrs. Mary, she has always tried to get us two together. Hmm one just doesn't know what could be going on within the minds of these people.

"Mrs. Mary, thank you for the breakfast. Now if you would excuse me, I'll go get that shower."

"Yes, Clay, you may be excused."

"Thank you, Mrs. Mary."

As I'm leaving to take my shower, I could feel the quietness as it overtook the room. I felt all their eyes following me out of the room and down the hallway. It's as if they couldn't wait for me to exit the kitchen before either of them said a word—one to the other. In all my time here, I've never felt such an eerier feeling like this one coming from them before.

After finishing my nice hot shower and brushing my teeth, I proceeded to get dressed for what I thought was going to be a long hard workday alongside Mr. John down at the motorcycle shop, but to my surprise, as I walked into the living room to where they all were sitting, Mr. John asks me, "Clay, how's your ankle feeling this morning?"

I still don't have any clue as to what is going on here, so I answer, "Sir, its feels fine."

"That is good to know, Clay, because I'm needing you and Lana...that if she doesn't mind going with you down to the shop and help my sons this morning."

As he is telling us this, I am beginning to think, *Now has this old man lost his mind? For this is something he'd never done before—asking me to supervise the shop this early in the morning.* Finding myself in total shock from his request, I say, "Well, what else am I to say other than sir, if that's what you're needing me to do, then that's just what I'll do...but, sir, there's just one thing I'm needing your instructions on."

"What would that be, Clay?"

"What am I to tell the two investigators who said they would be there at your shop at eight this morning?"

"Clay, I've told both of my sons what to tell them investigators if they show up, so there's no need for you or Lana to say anything."

"Yes, sir, you're the boss. I won't...or at least I try not to... say anything. But, Mr. John, if they start asking me any questions like they did before, I'll squeal like a hungry little piglet looking for his mother's tits."

"Oh no, you won't, Clay, because Lana will not let you. Will you, Lana?"

"Well now, Mr. John, it all depends on what they may threaten to do to us if we don't talk."

"Hmm, if they try to threaten you both, then tell them I'll be there sometime after lunch today, and that's all you need to tell them."

"Yes, sir. Mr. John, we can handle that, don't you think so? Oh, now where did Lana go?"

"Clay, I'm in the kitchen getting a glass of tea. Would you like one?"

"No, ma'am, I don't, but thanks for asking. I'm planning on stopping by the coffee shop to see Mary Ann. Now, Mr. John, what time are your sons going to show up at the shop?"

"Clay, I told them to be there no later than nine-thirty this morning. That should give you and Lana plenty of time to be there with the back doors open for them to back their trailers in. Now, like I've said, once I'm done taking care of my business at the bank, I'll be coming to shop to help load everything up. Now you both understand this is going to be an all-day job."

"Well, okay then. We'll see you when you get there, Mr. John. Let's get going, Lana."

"Clay, do you mind if I drive?"

"Lana, after the way you treated me last night, I'm not sure if I even want to ride while you are driving."

"Clay, I'm truly sorry about that. The only reason I asked is that I'm thinking of your ankle. Are you going to be able to drive?"

"Hmm, you may be right, Lana. Maybe you should do the driving just to be on the safe side, of course, but this time, please give me time to get in, okay?""Very funny, Clay. Thanks."

"You're welcome, but remember this—you got the life of my next wife in your hands...that if I ever find her."

"Clay, you're just full of it this morning, aren't you?"

"Lana, just what're you talking about 'I'm full of it'?"

"Clay, just forget I said anything. Now put on your seatbelt and hold on."

"Yes, ma'am, just don't you forget to stop at the coffee shop. I'm needing to see Mary Ann."

"Clay, is she the one who you were telling me about?"

"Yes, she's the one I told you about. Why don't you remember meeting her yesterday at the hospital?"

"Oh, that's right, I did. She's a nice-looking woman. *But I don't see what she sees in you.*"I'm sorry, Lana, I didn't understand you. Would you mind repeating that?"

"I said she's a nice-looking woman."

"Yes, Lana, she is, but after doing some deep soul searching of myself, for the life of me, I don't understand why an intelligent woman like her would say she's in love with me."

"Hmm."

"What was that, Lana?"

"Not a thing, Clay, I only took a deep breath...that's all it was."

"Oh, there for a second, Lana, I thought you were going to say something."

"Clay, why don't you just sit back and enjoy the ride? Now what are you looking for?"

"My pen and notebook...have you seen them?"

"They are on the back seat."

"Hmm, I can't reach them. Would you mind stopping so I can get them?"

"Only if you promise to stop talking while I'm driving."

Boy, has she gotten attitude all of a sudden. I sure hope her bedside manners are better with her patients.

"Clay, are you going to get them or not?"

"Yes, I am, Lana. Have you forgotten I can't just jump out with my bad ankle? Now why are you getting so impatient all at once?"

"Clay, I'm not going to explain my emotion. If you can't figure out, then that's on you."

Hmm, if that's doesn't sound just like a true woman, then I don't know what does. "Okay, Lana, I'm ready. We can go."

"Good."

*****

"Good morning, Sue, how're you, and is Mary Ann here?"

"I'm doing great...thanks for asking...and yes, Mary Ann is in the back cooking."

"Sue, would mind telling her I would like to speak with her for a minute please?"

"Clay, you should know by now that we're not allowed to have visitors when we're working."

"Oh, okay then, could you tell her that I need for her to bring me a cup of coffee?"

"Now, Clay, that won't work either."

"Well, fine then. Will you at least tell her for me to come by Mr. John's shop when she gets off work?"

"Yes, that I can do. Will there be anything else?"

"Yes, you can get me that cup of coffee, but make it to-go. Lana is waiting for me."

"Who is Lana?"

"Lana is Mrs. Mary's daughter. Just keep the change. I gotta go, and don't forget to tell Mary Ann what I said." *Boy, I just don't understand these women nowadays. They're nothing like the women of times past.*

*****

"Well, Clay, did you see Mary Ann?"

"No, Lana, I didn't. She was working as the cook this morning. Therefore, I told Sue to tell her that I needed to see her after she had gotten off work."

"Do you believe that she will come by the shop after work?"

"Yes, Lana...that if Sue doesn't forget to tell...her she will."

"Clay, I hope you don't mind me saying this. I took a look at what you had written this morning about the question you had asked Mr. John last night."

"Oh, you did, did you?"

"Yes, I did, and..."

"And what, Lana?"

"Well, Clay..."

"Look, Lana, either say what's on your mind or don't say anything at all."

"Clay, I would, but I'm not sure if you can handle what's on my mind."

Oh no, not now. It's still too early for this nonsense. "Look, Lana, you're really starting to sound just like Mr. John. Now is this going to be one of his constructive criticisms?"

"Clay, do you even know what a constructive criticism is or what it means?"

Hmm, maybe I do, maybe I don't, but I'm not going to let her know. Lana, are you insinuating that I don't have the ability to understand things like most people do?"

"Oh, no way, Clay, that's not at all what I meant."

"Well, Lana, that's what it sounded like to me."

Hmm, I should have just kept my big mouth shut. How do I apologize to him for my rude remarks? "Clay, it was very wrong of me to say that to you, and I'm even sorrier that I did. Will you please forgive me?"

"Oh heck, now, Lana, people have always treated me that way, so don't feel bad about your rudeness. I've gotten used to it. Now please tell me...what do you think about what I wrote?"

"I will if you promise me you will take it only as a constructive criticism."

"Lana, let me first say this, okay. If there's only one thing I could say I'm sure of that I've learned in my lifetime..."

"Yes, Clay, what would that be?"

"That would be that promises are easily broken. So please keep that in mind the next time you ask someone to make you a promise."

Hmm, now maybe he's not as dumb as Mr. John said he is, but I can't help to think otherwise after reading what he was writing. Wait now, perhaps I'm looking at the situation all wrong. Could it be he's...no, surely he's not dyslexic.

"Oh, Lana, are you going to tell me or not?"

"Yes, I'm going to tell you. Don't be getting so impatient. I'm doing some serious thinking here. Just drink your coffee."

Well, hmm, I'm starting to think you're overthinking what you're even thinking, or maybe she is, just a little.

"Clay, after searching deep into my mind as to what you wrote, have you ever been tested for dyslexia?"

Hmm, she has got me scratching my head as to how I'm going to answer that question. That's a tough one to answer—at least it is for me anyways.

"Well, Clay, have you or have you not? It is a simple yes-or-no question."

"Lana, it's not my intention to sound rude at all, but for me to answer your question at this stage of my life, does my answer really matter at all?"

"Clay, just for once in your life, will you please, *please* stop using that old excuse of being born tongue-tied and just listen to how you structure your language when you're speaking. It would help you out a lot. Wait, Clay, before you say anything, let me finish out what I'm saying, okay?"

"Sure, go ahead, speak your mind, Lana."

"When I read what you wrote, my first thought was man this sounds very beautiful. Then when I got back in the car and said what you did, your grammar sounded different and very awkward. That's why I asked you that question."

"Okay and?"

"Clay, that's all I got to say." *Well, one would hope so, because that was more than a mouthful even for me to say.*

"Lana, thank you for saying those words. They could be just ones that I needed to hear coming from a woman with a beautiful heart."

"Welcome."

"Do you have your story ready to tell?"

"Clay, what're you talking about now?"

"Lana, the two investigators are standing at the front door."

"Okay, let them stand there. I'm not doing anything wrong, and I must definitely don't have anything to say.""Oh, I see how this is going to play out. I'm the one they're going to question, aren't I?"

"Yeah, that's right. You're a big boy now."

"Gee, thanks, Lana."

*****

"Good morning. How are y'all doing this fine morning, sirs?"

"We're doing our best, thanks for asking."

"Clay, where is Mr. John this morning?"

"Hmm, well now, sir, he said for me to tell you both he would been here as soon as he's done handling his business at the bank, and that's all he said, I promise. Ain't that right, Lana?"

"Yeah, oh yeah, that's right, Clay. That's all I know of him saying."

"Okay, Clay, excuse us for just a second. I'm needing to have a talk with my partner. Mark, step over here. I want to tell you something."

"What is there for you to speak with me about, Peter?"

"Well, first thing, Mark, you're not to even use that tone of voice when speaking to me ever again. Do I make myself clear?"

"Oh yes, sir, very clear, sir, and I'm sorry. I'm wrong and you're right. It will never happen again."

"Good. Just don't let it happen again."

"Oh, yes, sir, it won't."

"Mark, if we start putting the squeeze on Clay, I bet he'll start squealing like a little piglet."

"Sure thing. How much you want to bet, Peter?"

"Oh, say hundred...that if you can afford to lose a hundred."

"You're on. Now put up or shut up."

*****

"Clay, did Mr. John, by any chance, say the name of the bank he's doing business at?"

"No, sir, not that I recall he didn't."

"Okay. Lana, do recall him saying the name of the bank?"

"Well, sir, I'm not sure if he ever did or not. You see, I'd step back into the kitchen to get a glass of tea for the road, so therefore, I didn't hear the full conversation that took place between him and Clay."

During the time she's telling her side of this story, I look at her, thinking not only does she knock me down with the bus, she's also running me over with it. Just what on this green earth is she thinking?"So, are we to believe he didn't say anything other than what you both said? Am I right about this?"

Clay thinks hard about it.

"You know we have ways of finding out the truth."

"Look now, Clay, if you know anything John said...and I meant anything other than what we agreed he had said he said...you best tell them."

Look at me...just look at me, Lana. Can you not see I've got sweat running down me like someone threw a five-gallon bucket of water on me? Gee whiz, just back off and let me think this over. "Oh, good, here comes his two sons. Maybe they can answer your question."

"Now, Clay, that's not going to work in this situation."

"But, sir, why not? Are they not his own sons, and does he not tell them everything?"

"Because the first thing, Clay, is we're not asking them. We're asking you right here and now. Now what else did John tell you to tell us? We're needing to know now?"

"Okay, okay already...I'll tell you, but first, can someone please get me a bath towel."

"Here's your towel, Clay, now start talking."

"Thank you so much, sir. May I sit down?"

"Clay, you're sitting down."

"Then, Lana, you being a nurse and all, why do I feel like I'm falling and my heart feels like it's going to jump right out of my chest?"

"Lana, you're a nurse. What's going on with him?"

"To be honest, I do believe he's having anxiety attack. Now that's just my observer's viewpoint."

"He's not having a heart attack, is he, Lana?"

"Without having a stethoscope, I can't be 100 percent accurate in my diagnosis. Although both a heart attack and anxiety attack almost have the same symptoms, but there is a difference between them. Clay, Clay! Look up at me. That's a good boy. Now open your mouth. I'm going to put this nitroglycerin sublingual tablet under your tongue, okay."

"Lana, is he going to be all right?"

"Mark, to be completely honest, I just don't know...but there's one thing I do know for certain."

"Ma'am, what would that be?"

"That you and your partner are responsible for causing this situation."

"Excuse me, Lana, I'm needing to talk with Peter. Peter, let's step outside and talk."

"Yes, sir."

"Howdy."

"Hello."

"Hmm, I wonder who they are. Lana, how's it looking for Clay?"

"Mork, please hold down your voice, and don't you dare say that I've to say anything while those two are still here."

"Lana! All I've asked is how's Clay doing. Is he or is he not okay?"

"Come here. Come a little closer."

"Hmm, you don't say?"

"Yes, that's right, Mork, and if this ever gets out, Clay and I will know who told."

"Look, Lana, that's just between you and Clay. I'm going back to work, for I know nothing."

"Great job, Lana. Now will you please get me a glass of water?"

"Yes, Clay, I will."

Man, I wish Mr. John would hurry up and get here."Clay, here's your water."

"Lana, just sprinkle some on my forehead before Mark and Peter get back in here."

"Look, Clay, don't you think you're taking this a little too far?"

"Well! No, Lana. Have you forgotten that they are the ones who made a bet that they could get me to squeal like a piglet on Mr. John's whereabout?"

"No, I haven't forgotten, but still..."

"Now look, Lana, if you're starting to feel a little guilty, then don't. If I was a biting man, which I'm not, I be willing to say they themselves are now sweating within those four-hundred-dollar tailormade suits."

"Clay, do you really think they are?"

"Lana, I'm not a biting man for no reason."

"Hmm, do what?"

"Quickly here they come. Sprinkle my face."

Quietness fills the room.

"Miss Lana, Mr. Clay, after we've talked everything over, we then talked with Mr. John's son Mork, and he confirmed both of your stories."

"Well, Mr. Mark, isn't that what Clay asked both of you to do in the first place?"

"Yes, ma'am, he did."

"Then, Mr. Peter, why did you both badger him in the way you did? Don't you know that you could've caused him to have a heart attack?"

"Well, ma'am, you see..."

"Oh! Don't you dare 'well, ma'am' me."

Hmm, I'm starting to think now this woman most definitely got some go-getter in her from the way she handles these two guys.

"Miss Lana, we both understand your anger, and you have every right to be, but at the same time..."

"Excuse me my anger."

"Please, Miss Lana, let me finish my sentence, okay? We hope that you understand we're just doing our job. Mr. Clay, we hope you'll be all right. Let's be on our way, Peter. We've gotten all the information we came for."

"Oh, wait, now you two aren't going to leave here without first apologizing to Clay for putting him through the torment that you did."

"What do you say, Peter, do we apologize for doing our job or not?"

"Sir, you're the highest-ranking officer. That's your call, not mine."

"Okay then, Peter, you apologize. I'll be waiting in the car."

"Ya, right, ain't that like and officer to leave behind the lowest rank to do all the dirty work. Ma'am, Clay sir, I'm very sorry for the way Mark and I treated you both here today. Ma'am, I hope you don't think I'm being to forward with you, but can I get your phone number?"

"Peter, sorry that would be a no, but thank you for doing the work of a real man. You may go in peace now."

"Hmm, wow, Lana, that was a great performance."

"Oh, Clay, why don't you just lay there and hush up. Putting up with this has given me a headache."

Not in all my days have I even met a woman quite like her other than my mother, of course. She showed me that no matter what may come her way, she has the courage to face it with nerves of steel even when I myself became breathless.

"Okay, Clay, they have left the premises. You can come out and help us."

"My ankle is hurting me, Mork. I'm going to stay in here and keep it elevated for a little while longer, okay?"

"Yeah, right, Clay. I've forgotten about your bad ankle."

"That's all right, Mork. Lana is on her way out to help you with the work."

"Clay, it's not Lana's place to be doing this kind of work."

"Mork, it's all right. I don't mind helping you guys out. Besides, it will keep me from having to put up with him."

"I heard that, Lana."

"Good, Clay, I'm glad you did."

"Well! Fine then. I love you just as much. Just by the way, what time is it getting to be? It's only half past eleven, man. Time sure seems to have come to a standstill."

"Clay! Why are you laying on the floor in my office?"

Uh-oh, that sounded like Mr. John. "Hello, Mr. John, how did things go at the bank?"

"Clay, I'm the one who's asking the question here. Why are you laying on the floor and not out there helping Mork, Joe, and Lana?"

"Hmm, wait now. There's no need in getting all upset, Mr. John. Please let me explain what has happened here."

"Clay, there's no need, for Mork and Lana have already told me, and I don't see that as an excuse for you to be laying around."

"That's just fine then, Mr. John. I'll just take my bad ankle on out there and get hurt all over again if that's the way you feel, and there's one thing more..."

"Yeah, what would that be?"

"Sir, I hope you got some of the best insurance in this small town to pay my medical bills because it will be on you to do so."

"Hmm, if he does get hurt, that would mean Mary and I couldn't start our traveling. Clay, why don't you stay in here until Mary Ann comes pick you up?"

"Sir, thank you. I'll do as you've said and sit here and keep out of y'all way."

5:45, Monday evening"Hello! Mary Ann, I'm sure glad to see you. I wasn't sure if Sue was going to tell you to come by after work today."

"Clay, don't you dare ever doubt my best friend Sue."

I'm like feeling within myself. Now I don't know what has happened to these people today. It's like I've woken up on a completely different planet where everyone looks and talks the same but acts t-totally different than they did the day before this one. "Yes, Mary Ann, you're right. I should have not second-guessed Miss Sue like that. I'm sorry."

"Clay, you should be feeling sorry...sorry to the point where you should apologize to Sue for not believing in her. Let me ask you this—have you ever had someone not to believe in you?"

Uh-hmm, I wonder does she really want to know that answer. "Mary Ann, there have been times in my life that some of the people who I've met along the way didn't, and I'll leave it at that. Now would you mind stopping at the beach? There's something I would like to discuss with you."

"Clay, you oughta know I don't mind stopping at the beach. Have you forgotten it's one of my favorite places to be when I'm with the person I love."

Boy, you're talking about being on an emotional roller-coaster ride. Well, that's the very feeling I'm having right now. This ride started earlier this morning with the eerier feelings filling the kitchen as I finished eating breakfast before taking a shower.

"Clay, you're not acting like yourself."

"Whatever do you mean, Mary Ann?"

"Clay, you got quiet all of a sudden. Now would you mind telling what's on your mind?"

"Mary Ann, I'm not sure just where to start this conversation."

"Why don't you try telling me what it is that you would like to talk with me about and just let the conversation develop from there?"

Boy, I'm thinking now is she not showing off her college intelligence or what? "Mary Ann, this is what's been going through my mind since we last talked."

"Yes, Clay, what would that be going through that mind of yours?"

"Uh-hmm, stop that, for I've been trying, for the life of me, to determine what the difference is between true love and lust. See, what you've gone and done to me, Mary Ann, I can't even think straight."

"Maybe if I do this, Clay, it will help you get back on track with you train of thought."

"Oh, you're right, Mary Ann, that does help. Thank you."

"What I was about to say is how does one tell the differences between true love and lust?"

"Say what?"

"Mary Ann, you do have a certified college degree in human behavior. Therefore, I would think you, of all people, would be able to help me to reach a conclusion on such a great matter as this one."

"Clay, how old are you?"

"Mary Ann, I don't see where my age has anything to do with this subject although you've asked, so I'll tell you this much. I'm old enough to know the difference between a man and a woman, and that's more that some grown adults who hold high office in the land. Wait now...how did we get off subject?"

"Sorry. Apparently I asked you the wrong question, so let me ask you this question. At what age did you find yourself looking at females as an opposite sex?"

"Look now, Mary Ann, I know that you know we both are grown adults here. Now tell me—why are you asking these kinds of questions?"

"Clay, you've asked for my help. Now do you want my help or not?"

"Yes, I'd like your help, but I'm not understanding why these types of questions."

"Clay, the first thing I'm trying to get you to understand is how lust works."

Hmm, I'm thinking she just might be on to something here with these questions, so I'll just ask her one of my own to see if I'm right or not. "Mary Ann, please tell me that this's not going to be a lesson about adolescence? Because if it is, I'll go ahead and tell you I already know just how the birds and the bees play."

"Oh, so you do...do you!"

"Yes, ma'am...at least at one time I thought I did, but you see in this world in which we're living in today, one can't be that sure of themselves anymore."

*****

"Hey now, Clay, hey. You need to wake up. We're at the beach."

"Hmm, what...we're where? Oh, we're at beach. Man, that was some dream I was having."

"Yes, it must have been, Clay. I just wish I've had my tape recorder with me."

"Why is that?"

"So I could've recorded the conversation you were having."

"Mary Ann, are you saying I was talking in my sleep?"

"Yes, you were."

"Then what was I talking about?"

"Understand I only got one side of the conversation, and it sounded to me like you trying to get someone to help you learn the difference between true love and lust."

"Are you sure I wasn't talking to you, Mary Ann?"

"Clay, the way in which you were talking, let's just say you were dreaming for now."

"Okay then, you can be the boss."

"Clay, are you feeling all right? You're not being yourself?"

"Yes, I'm feeling fine, for there's no pain coming from this bad ankle anymore."

"How many of those pain pills did you take?"

"I only took enough to stop the pain. Is that not what the doctor gave them to me for—to stop the pain—and that's just what I did. Hmm...that's right, stop the pain. I'm feeling no more pain, that I ain't. Now give me kiss since there's ain't more pain to feel."

"I'm taking you back to the house and put you to bed so that you can sleep this off."

"Hm, what, no kiss since that ain't no more pain?"

"Clay, just lay there and sleep off those pain pills."

Good, then I didn't need a kiss from any old way.

*****

"Hello, Mrs. Mary. I'm calling to let you know Clay is going to be staying with me tonight."

"Mary Ann, is everything all right with Clay?"

"Yes, ma'am. He just took one too many of his pain pills. I just put him in bed so he could sleep it off."

"Thank you, Mary Ann, for letting me know so that I wouldn't be worried about his whereabouts tonight. Good night."

*****

"John, did I not ask you and Lana both to keep an eye on Clay?"

"We both did. Now what's your worry, Mary?"

"That was Mary Ann calling to tell me that Clay took way too many pain pills and now he's talking out of his head."

"Hmm, Mother, I wonder how she can tell he's doing that, for every time I've talked with him, he's sounded that way."

"Yes, Mary, for I to would like to know the answer to that."

"Well, Lana, I've never in all my days heard such a profound statement come from you...but as for you, John, I understand, so therefore, I'm not even going to try answering either of you. Now good night."

"Good night, Mother. Love you."

"Yeah, right. I love you too, Lana."*5:20 a.m. Tuesday*I'm woken from my deep sleep by this strong urge to visit the restroom. As my feet touch the floor, my arms rising over my head, I begin to stand up, when suddenly a sharp pain shut up my left leg. I then sit back down on the side of the bed only to realize that I'm not at Mr. John's house.

I find myself asking, "If I'm not at Mr. John's, then just where am I?"

As I try to think back to who the last person I was with, Mary Ann comes to mind; but still not sure, I turn, looking over my left shoulder to see if she's lying in the bed, and she's not. I reach for the light that is sitting on the nightstand beside me only to knock it off the nightstand. I hear this sweet voice coming through the air from the room next to me, asking, "Clay, are you all right?"

In my disbelief, it's the voice of no other than Miss Sue. I let a few seconds pass to regain my composure from the shock of hearing her voice, but before I could even get a word out, there they both stand within the doorway—Miss Sue and Mary Ann.

"Clay, are you all right?"

"Yes, Sue, I'm all right. I just need to get to the restroom."

"Clay, I see that you've knocked the light off the nightstand."

"Yes, Mary Ann, and I'm sorry about that. I know there's no excuse for it, but not knowing my way around in your home at night, I hope you understand accidents will occur."

"Do you need one of us to help you to the restroom?"

"Yes, please."

"Sue, would you get the broom and dustpan while I help him to the restroom?"

"No, Mary Ann, you get the broom and dustpan, and I'll help him to the restroom."

"Hey, look now. It doesn't matter who gets them. I'm needing to get to the restroom, or you both be needing more than just a broom and dustpan alright. Now you both can help me to where the restroom is before a much bigger accident occurs."

"Okay, Clay, just hold your business. We'll get you there."

"Thanks, Mary Ann, and you as well, Sue. Mary Ann, once I'm done, could we finally have that discussion from yesterday?"

"What would that discussion be about?"

"Oh, Sue, it's knowing the differences between true love and lust?"

"Clay! You do realize it's only five-forty in the morning, right?"

"Well, Sue, that only means it's just twenty minutes before six. Now if I was at Mr. John's, I be already up eating breakfast, and just by the way...how did I end up sleeping here?"

"Clay, are you saying that you don't remember why you slept here tonight?"*Hmm, now this question here does need some serious thinking over before I can answer it, but in the meantime, my answer is no—just to see what their reaction is going to be.* "No, Mary Ann, Sue, can't say that I've got a clue as to why I slept here."

"Okay, Clay, just which one of us do you think knows why you slept here?"

"Wait, are you two trying to pull some kind of trick here, Mary Ann?"

"Come now, Clay, why would you even think something like that about us?"

That's a good question coming from Sue.

www.ingramcontent.com/pod-product-compliance
Lightning Source LLC
Chambersburg PA
CBHW040842010826
48978CB00012BB/866